PARIS-CHIEN

adventures of an ex-pat dog

WRITTEN AND ILLUSTRATED BY

Jackie Clark Mancuso

LA LIBRAIRIE PARISIENNE

Hi. My name is Hudson.

My mom is a writer and we've come to live in Paris for a year.

I'm pretty excited because she said it's a really cool place for dogs.

We live in a fancy neighborhood called the 7th arrondissement, whatever that means.

I can't wait to meet some French dogs.

My mom says Parisians take their dogs everywhere, so I'll never get left at home.

They take them to work.

Like this guy who greets people
at a shoe store on Boulevard Raspail.

They take them to get baguettes.

And haircuts.

Even to cafes and restaurants,
where they often get the best tables.

But everyone's
so busy
going places
that I haven't
been able
to make
any friends.

We went to
a park, but
there was a sign.

No dogs allowed.

Are you
kidding me?

...I couldn't understand them.
Oh great. I thought all dogs spoke Dog.

They only speak French.

I'll never make any friends.

I hate Paris.

I want to
go home.

I don't think so, Huddie.

I have an idea.

My teacher is Madame Vera.
She's a French poodle.

One day at recess I met Warren.
He's an "ex-pat," an American dog
who's lived here a long time.

He's slow learning French, but he
sure knows his way around Paris.

He takes me to new places to smell stuff.
My favorite is the sausage man.

One day we walked
really far and
ended up at
Marché d'Aligre,
his favorite
market.

Everyone was speaking French, but now I could actually understand some of what they were saying!

Now I *really* want to learn more words.

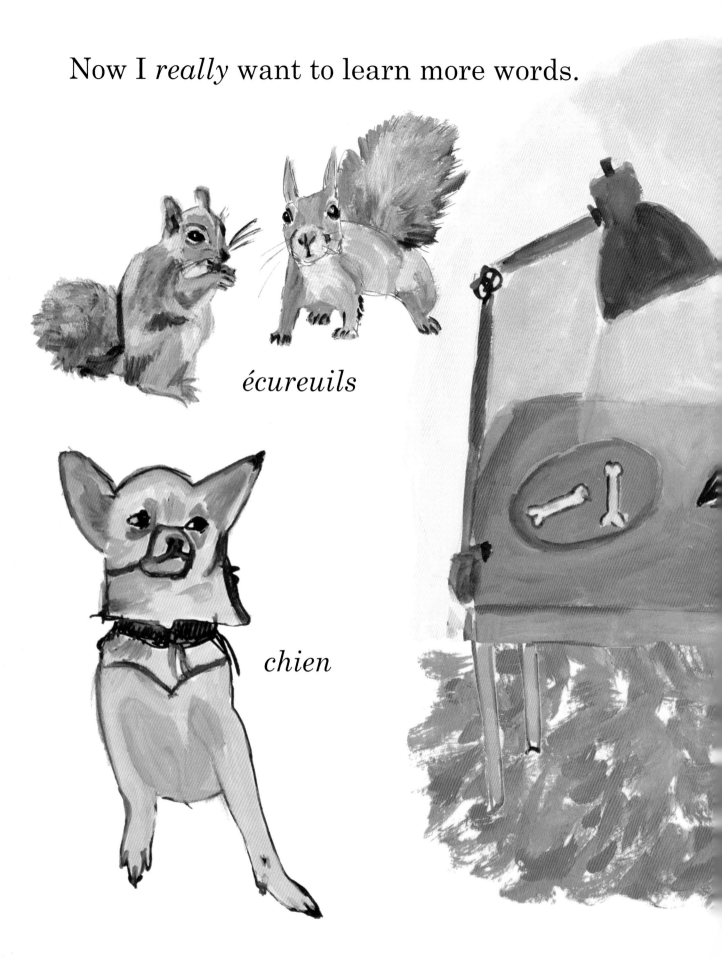

écureuils

chien

oiseau

chat

The next time
I saw a dog
at the park,
I started talking
to him, and he
understood me!

Now Gustave
and I are friends.

Then I met Leo.
He's a
Siberian
husky.

He's very cool.

I'm making lots of friends, like Marion, Jean-Jacques, Beatrice and Emile.

I even have a girlfriend.
Her name is Françoise.

I asked her to play, and she said
"Oui."

But in Paris you say it like this:
"*Waaaaaaaaay!*"

Paris *is* a cool place
when you have friends.

I'm becoming a real Parisian.

I mean **PARIS-CHIEN !**

FIN